D0992573

HOTTER 'N PECOS

And Other West Texas Lies

BOBBY D. WEAVER

Foreword by Barry Corbin
illustrations by
Boots Reynolds

TEXAS TECH UNIVERSITY PRESS

Copyright © 2010 by Bobby D. Weaver
Foreword and illustrations copyright © 2010 Texas Tech University Press

All rights reserved. No portion of this book may be reproduced in any form or by any
means, including electronic storage and retrieval systems, except by explicit
prior written permission of the publisher. Brief passages excerpted
for review and critical purposes are excepted.

This book is typeset in Scala. The paper used in this book meets the minimum
requirements of ANSI/NISO Z39.48-1992 (R1997). ∞

Designed by Kasey McBeath

Illustrated by Boots Reynolds

Library of Congress Cataloging-in-Publication Data
Weaver, Bobby.
Hotter 'n pecos and other west Texas lies / Bobby D. Weaver ; foreword by Barry Corbin.
p. cm.
Summary: "Collected tales, some taller than others, offer glimpses into Texas west
of the hundredth meridian. Four parts—Working in the Oil Patch, Riding the Range,
Down on the Farm, and Weather—humorously reflect on the nature of West
Texans living in an environment that is "Hotter 'n Pecos""—Provided by publisher.
ISBN 978-0-89672-703-8 (pbk. : alk. paper) 1. Texas, West—Anecdotes. 2. Petroleum
industry and trade—Texas, West—Anecdotes. 3. Ranch life—Texas, West—Anecdotes.
4. Texas, West—Climate—Anecdotes. I. Title.
F386.6.W43 2010
976.4'9—dc22   2009053349

Printed in the United States of America
10 11 12 13 14 15 16 17 18 / 9 8 7 6 5 4 3 2 1

Texas Tech University Press
Box 41037 | Lubbock, Texas 79409-1037 USA
800.832.4042 | ttup@ttu.edu | www.ttup.ttu.edu

For Jim, Roz, and Rob
who have had to put up with
these yarns all their lives

CONTENTS

FOREWORD

I come from a long line of farmers, ranchers, fiddlers, and storytellers. In the 1920s, my great-grandfather was ranching near Lampasas,
Texas, when he decided he wanted to raise cotton. Well, sir, he looked all
over Texas and finally decided on a farm in Dawson County about eight
miles east of Lamesa. As you probably know, La Mesa is the Spanish
name for "the table" and it was the perfect name for that country. The
whole area around there is as flat as a huge dinner table and as dry as
the Mojave Desert most of the time. But when great-granddad arrived
there, they'd had a couple of years of good rain and it looked like the Gar-
den of Eden. Needless to say, after he bought the place, in about 1927,
everything dried up.

Great-granddad died not long after that and my granddad, L. E.
Corbin, farmed the place until his health failed in the early 1960s. Some
of my most cherished memories come from the 1940s and 1950s, sitting
on the front porch of the house Granddad built himself and listening to
the stories he and his friends told about living close to nature on unfor-
giving land.

In this book, Bobby Weaver brings back that time vividly. For those of
you who had the advantage of growing up in rural West Texas, sitting
around the gin or domino parlor and listening to the old men tell stories
through fogs of Bull Durham tobacco smoke, this book will stir those
half-forgotten memories to burn brightly again. For those of you who

didn't have that advantage, get ready to step into the world of the oil patch roughneck, the cowman, the farmer, and all the other unforgettable people that are part and parcel of what we call West Texas.

Just to get you started in the right frame of mind, I'll tell you a little story that is (mostly) true. My father, Kilmer B. Corbin, was raised on that Dawson County farm. He rode horseback to school and hated every minute of it. He couldn't wait to get off that farm. So he became a lawyer. After he got his license to practice law, he drove out to Granddad's place and waited beside the road at the turnrow of the field Granddad was plowing. When Granddad got to Dad he got off the tractor and rolled a smoke and asked what he was doing there in the middle of the day. Dad said, "Well, sir, I just wrote a check on your account for twenty-five dollars. I've announced to run for county judge." He was twenty-one years old at the time. Granddad looked at him for a second, took another draw on his cigarette, and started laughing. He laughed until he was in a full-blown coughing fit. When he finally settled down, he said, "Son, if you get elected to that office, I'm gonna run for president next election." The joke was on Granddad, though; my dad won, served two terms, then was twice elected state senator.

Well, enough of my yammerin'. It's time for you to sit down in a cafe with a cup of hot coffee and listen to a few old guys with work-calloused hands that are missing some fingers, or to sit on the top rail of a loading pen with broke-down, busted-up old cowhands and learn something about life in West Texas. Saddle up! You're in for a good ride.

Barry Corbin
Fort Worth, Texas

INTRODUCTION

My wife says that Texans are the most truthful people in the world, so truthful, she asserts, that we ofttimes tell more truth than actually exists. I take that as a compliment, even though she—being from New Mexico—probably meant it as something of a slur. Our approach to truth helps define us as a people. We love a good story. Besides, it puts me in fairly esteemed company. In his introduction to *Coronado's Children,* no less than the legendary J. Frank Dobie declared something to the effect that there was never a story that could not bear improvement.

As long as I can remember, my family has shared yarns relating to our life in the Lone Star State. My Uncle "Bud" (I was a man grown before I knew that his name was Johnny Wells) was one of my favorite storytellers. He usually began with something like, "Once when we were baling hay down on the old Jones place." Then he would turn to somebody and say something like, "You recollect them, don't you? They were the ones that lived down on Owl Creek and had that tongue-tied kid nobody could ever understand." Then he would launch into a tale that usually had a humorous bent. Old Uncle Bud is gone now, but I never think of him without recalling those dark nights out on the side gallery of the old farmhouse and the stories he swapped with the other grownups. It makes me realize how many West Texas yarns I've stored up on my own that might be worth sharing, or at least worth improving—especially if you know something of the good folk of that part of the state.

The year I turned twelve, my family moved to the West Texas oil fields. My dad was a tank builder. So, as soon as I got big enough to tote iron, I went out with the crew. I spent the next twenty years working in the oil patch. When it finally dawned on me that I was not going to get rich in a pair of greasy overalls (I have always been a little slow in certain respects), I enrolled in college. Attending college was so much easier than working for a living that I settled in for ten years or so until they gave me a doctorate just to be rid of me. For the next twenty years, ten of which I spent in Oklahoma, I labored in a variety of museums (Want to swap tales about doing hard time? You're on!).

At best, it's been a spotty career that yielded the material for this book. I must confess that I did glance at a document or two for a couple of the yarns. It is true that many of the stories are semi-autobiographical—that is to say they actually happened to me, sort of. I suppose, however, that all those West Texans I worked for, with, and against over the years are really the ones who deserve credit. A colorful lot, they illuminate every nuance of these stories, especially those twists that thanks to Uncle Bud, I've learned to appreciate as humorous, at least in retrospect.

It is also true that most of these narratives are tall tales. Some are just not as tall as others. Some are character sketches, and some are stories shared with me by those I met along the way. But every one of them contains some grain of truth. I must admit that some of those grains are very small while others are boulder-sized, and some of them are the absolute gospel truth (okay, at least as I envision the truth). In the interest of full disclosure (all right, to appease my New Mexico-bred wife) and to prepare you for what lies ahead, I offer an illustrative example. You decide whether it's wise to read further.

How Tales Grow Tall

A number of years ago, I was working as a curator at a well-known Texas museum. One day shortly after lunch, while operating a table saw, I suffered an accident in which I lost the vision of my right eye. Some of my fellow workers transported me about four blocks to the local hospital where the resident physician stabilized the projectile protruding from my eye and called an ambulance to transport me to a larger facility some twenty miles away where they performed surgery. I remained in the hospital for about a week and convalesced at home for more than a month before returning to work. Those are the basic facts of my accident.

About ten years later, long after I had moved on to other employment, I was back in the area visiting old friends when one of them launched into the story of my accident. That is when I learned about mythmaking. He related how I was working late in the evening one weekend when nobody else was around. The accident occurred pretty much as it happened in reality. Then I left the premises, carefully reset the alarm system so the building would be safe, drove myself to the hospital, and admitted myself to the emergency room where I had my operation. I returned home the following day and reported to work as usual on Monday morning with this huge patch over my bad eye.

When the story was finished, he turned to me and inquired if that was not the way it happened. All I could do was nod my head yes.

And that, my friends, is what you call a yarn with legs.

One
WORKING IN THE
OIL PATCH

Oil-field hands are a different breed from most industrial workers. The transient nature of their labor has largely thwarted unionization and cultivated a fierce independence. At the same time the difficult and often dangerous nature of their work has always attracted a younger work force from the small towns, farms, and ranches of Texas. That these factors combine to paint oil-field workers as adventurous and reckless may also explain their reputation for drinking and fighting. That reputation may be exaggerated, but I do recall an incident that seems to support it. Back when I was tanking out in West Texas, I worked with two brothers, Donald and Marshall, who loved to fight. They each stood well over six feet and tipped the scales at a smidgeon over the two-hundred-pound mark. Nobody in his right mind would challenge them, which tended to leave them bored and just a bit cranky. Then they came up with the idea of bait. Naturally, I was the bait: all 135 pounds of me. My role was to make obnoxious advances to some girl in whatever dance hall we happened to find ourselves. When the scuffle started, as it was sure to do, the brothers would rush in and take over. It worked too, except for the time that they decided to keep on drinking and let me go it alone. That was also when I decided to retire from the ring with only one major defeat on my record.

GRADUATION NIGHT

Graduation night in Wink was always a big deal. All the seniors, decked out in mortarboards and long black robes, paraded one by one up on the auditorium stage to receive their diplomas. The whole town turned out for the event. Afterwards there was a dance at the gym and later on a midnight supper, served this particular year at the First Baptist Church. Some graduates slipped off after the dance in favor of one of the local honkytonks to experience earthier pleasures. But Bill took no part in any of the festivities beyond receiving his diploma.

By eleven P.M. he was sitting on the front stoop of his folk's house with a sack lunch in his clenched right hand. Beside him, rolled in a neat bundle, was a new pair of overalls, a clean work shirt, a pair of steel-toed Red Wing work boots, and two pairs of canvas Boss Walloper work gloves. He was waiting for the crew car to arrive and take him out to Consolidated's Rig #4 where he would be working backup tongs as a roughneck.

Like a lot of kids born and reared in the oil patch, Bill considered a good-paying roughnecking job the pinnacle of success. By the time the graveyard crew picked him up, he was about as excited as any eighteen-year-old could get, except for maybe that time he scored the winning touchdown against Pyote in district playoffs. At last he was getting some-where in life. He was going to be a man and have bragging rights in the local beer joints, just like all the other oil-field hands he knew.

After relieving the evening tour crew, the driller sent Bill and the lead tong man down into the cellar to finish installing the blowout preventer. The tong man, of course, had already been ribbing Bill pretty hard about finishing high school. As they made their way down beneath the rig floor, he started in again. This time he questioned the intelligence of any high school graduate who went around with a pair of Boss Wallopers stuffed in his hip pocket.

It took about thirty minutes to get everything arranged so they could lower the heavy blowout preventer into place. Bill was brushing some dirt off the base flange when it happened. They never did figure out just what caused it, but at that very moment the preventer fell with a crash. Bill managed to jerk his hands partially back before the massive hunk of iron smashed the ends of his Boss Wallopers flat as a pancake. The kid just stood there for what seemed an eternity, his face losing color as red began to stain the fingers of both gloves. Finally, he eased his hands out of the gloves and fearfully inspected all ten of his digits. Incredibly they were all there except for the tips of both middle fingers, which were slightly nipped. That was the last time the crew saw Bill.

Four years later, almost to the day, graduation night rolled around again. Once again Bill participated, this time receiving his hard-won diploma on a college campus. Beneath his graduation robe, however, firmly tucked in his hip pocket, was a pair of fingerless Boss Wallopers— a reminder of what he had missed by leaving the patch.

THE BOLL WEEVIL

The minute I saw him standing there in that pool hall, looking around like a lost soul in purgatory, I knew that he was just the type of hand we needed. He wore a size five hat and a size fifty jumper. Clearly he was fresh off the farm, with little enough sense but to put in a hard day's work. In a more civilized line of work he might be called green as a gourd, but in parlance of the patch, he was the quintessential "boll weevil." The driller hired him on the spot, and he went out with us on the graveyard tour that night.

That boll weevil sure lived up to our expectations. He worked like a mule, but like all new hands he tried to do everything the hard way. It took a while for him to learn to let the machinery do the heavy work. In the interim we played just about every prank that we knew. That included sending him to look for left-handed monkey wrenches, sets of sky hooks, and even pairs of pipe stretchers. Eventually, despite his hat size, he began to question everything we told him.

Just the same, the kid was so proud of his new profession that as soon as he drew wages, he rushed out to buy a brand new aluminum hard hat that he buffed to a brilliant luster. Even the tool pusher avowed that the hat shone like "a diamond in a goat's behind." It was at least as shiny as a gas flare on a dark night and soon egged us on to our finest prank.

Before long the derrick man engaged the weevil in a heated discussion

as to who was the better coordinated. Finally the weevil was persuaded to agree to a contest the derrick man called cutting the line. They would lay a short length of cotton cord on a 2x4 and see who could swing a hatchet to cut closest to a given spot.

The driller was drafted to act as judge and supreme arbitrator. He declared that the contestants should remove their hard hats because the safety chapeaus might impede accuracy of aim. With that the adversaries whacked away, and the judge, with plenty of commentary from the rest of the crew, eventually called the contest a draw. After much discussion it was decided that a better test would be for the contestants to have another go at it blindfolded. They flipped a coin, and the weevil won the honor of going first. Once the weevil's blindfold was firmly in place, the crew quietly replaced the length of line with his new hard hat. The unwitting weevil drew back and delivered a mighty blow exactly on the designated spot. That hat was never the same, and it took some hard persuasion to keep the derrick man from serious injury that day.

It must have been a couple of months after the kid hired on when things reached a tipping point. He was tightening some loose bolts with a large wrench when the tool slipped out of his hand and fell down the well bore. That was not a good thing, because no oil-well bit can drill through a foreign metal object at the bottom of the hole. There was nothing to do but fish out the wrench from more than 3,000 feet below. It took a lot maneuvering over the next three days, but finally we got the job done.

The minute that battle-scarred old wrench surfaced, the driller handed it to the kid and made him hold it. Then he commenced to scream and holler at the top of his lungs about how he had never been so "weevil bit" in his entire twenty years in the oil patch. The driller raved and ranted on and on until I guess he just ran out of cuss words and told the kid he was fired. The kid never said a word. As he stood there staring the driller straight in the eye, a peculiar little grin began to play around the corners of his mouth. When the tirade finally ended, the kid turned, dropped the ruined wrench right back into the well bore, and walked off the job.

At that point we all agreed that he was no longer a boll weevil.

BUCK THE TANK SETTER

Buck was a mean old SOB, on that we were all agreed. He stood a gaunt 6'3" and always sported a scraggly growth of gray whiskers that accentuated a deep scar along his right cheek bone. One hand compared Buck's unusually nasal voice, almost always raised in anger, to the cry of a wounded wart hog. Hard to please fails to describe his temperament. In short, Buck was the model graduate of the patch's screaming and hollering school of management.

I first laid eyes on him in the fall of '55. We were working on a Humble lease out of Snyder. Our crew was setting two 500-barrel bolted tanks, and Buck's crew had a similar job about a quarter mile down the road. Even as we drove up and began to change into our work clothes, we could hear him screaming at his hands. Evidently his indelicate language upset one lad who decided to rearrange the setter's countenance. Well sir, one thing led to another and in short order the disgruntled employee had enough knuckle knots that he returned to work without further argument.

Over time I got to know old Buck better. I worked for him occasionally when my crew was not busy. The man had a number of peculiarities. He always saucered his morning coffee, and you could hear him slurping it from any point across the greasy spoon cafes where we always ate. Then there was the matter of his cars. Buck drove Packards. When they ceased manufacturing them in the late 1950s he bought two right off the showroom floor and stored them so he could have a decent car to drive for the rest of his life. All the hands doubted they would last that long. For one thing, Buck was too mean to ever die. For another, he was hell on everything he drove.

One reason it was so difficult to work for Buck was that you never knew when he would change the rules. Once Leroy Bollier and I worked for him for about two weeks running. During that time we must have built close to 300 feet of walkway. Knowing how particular old Buck was, we got it clear the first day just how he wanted that walkway built. Everything went fine for the first ten or twelve days. Then he decided that we were not doing the job right even though we had not altered our assembly technique in any way. He threw a real fit and went into a tirade that lasted all afternoon. In the interest of peace, we let the question drop. The next morning Buck pulled up in front of my house about five as usual. By the time I got out to the curb all that was there were my work clothes in a neat pile. Most times that was how you knew Buck had fired you.

The day Buck finally got his comeuppance, it was at the hands of a most unlikely source—an old-timer tankie with a serious drinking problem. No matter how badly the setter treated him, that old wino just took it without protest. Then one day the two of them were on a job out west of Lovington, New Mexico, up on what we called the Old Hagerman Road. It was a long way from anywhere, and they were there all alone. About midmorning Buck had a tank up on one of those big old Simplex house jacks while he reached underneath trying to insert a missing bolt. The jack kicked out and the tank fell, pinning both the setter's arms underneath. Buck let out one of those wounded wart-hog screams, which brought the old man running. When he arrived, there lay old Buck with both arms firmly pinned into the soil. Quickly the old man took stock of the situation. There was no blood. When he asked Buck if anything felt broken, the setter hollered, "Hell no, I'm just stuck here."

"Are you sure you just can't get loose, that you're not bad hurt?" the old man asked.

Buck's affirmation spewed out in his inimitable string of curses, whereupon the old guy ambled back to the work trailer and carefully selected an eight- or ten-foot length of two-inch rubber gasket material, which he folded over a couple of times as he returned to Buck's side. Then he proceeded to give old Buck a really good spanking. After that he changed casually into his street clothes and drove the Packard the fifty miles back into Lovington. That evening, after a nice nap, he called the company man and told him where he could find Buck.

They say that when the company man finally got old Buck loose, he was so hoarse from cussing that his voice was little more than a squeak. To the best of my knowledge that tank setter never spoke of the incident, and we damned well never brought it up to him.

THE DAY OLD WHITEY QUIT

Old Whitey was pretty much a legend in West Texas's Permian Basin when I was growing up. Stories about him were legion, and most revolved around his prickly personality. For example, there was the time he was still changing clothes when the evening tour driller he was relieving chose to offer a derogatory remark. At the moment Whitey had his right thumb hooked in the right strap of his overalls. Without hesitating he punched the other driller right on the chin and knocked him cold. It was not until later that he discovered that he'd broken his thumb when he swung. By the time Whitey's tour was over, his whole hand was swollen, but all we knew to do was put ice on it and hope for the best. Whitey never missed a minute of work, but the evening tour driller quit rather than face a return match.

Then there was the time Whitey was working derricks on a deep well up in Gaines County. He had been drunk for about a week or so, and when he went out that particular night he was hung over and not in the best of moods. No sooner was the crew on the job than the driller decided to change bits. This meant that they would have to make a round trip; that is, they would remove and reinsert 5,000 feet of drill pipe. As Whitey would have to handle every stand of pipe both ways, he determined to persuade the driller that the bit was not all that dull. The discussion grew heated and ended with the driller lying prone and semiconscious while Whitey finished the shift as acting driller. As luck would have it, they entered a thick formation of salt, and Whitey set a footage drilling record that night. But that didn't stop the tool pusher from firing him the next morning.

Despite Whitey's many indiscretions, the old driller had his lighter moments. Once when he was drilling for some outfit west of Odessa he arrived at midnight and relieved the evening tour driller who was just starting to pull a drill stem test. This meant that they would relieve the mud pressure in the hole and allow the well to flow to see if they had a showing of oil or gas. As the weight of the mud decreased, the drill pipe began to rise out of the hole of its own accord. This meant that the gas pressure was out of control. They were about to have a blowout—a situation all drilling personnel fear. They say that the drilling log Whitey kept that night had three entries. The first said, "12:00 relieved evening tour crew." The second said, "12:30–1:00 well blew out and running away from rig." The third read, "1:00–8:00 walking back to rig."

Back in August of '53 Whitey was the daylight driller on National's Rig #8 when new technology got the best of him. They had just completed the second of four contracted wells on a lease down below Midland, just west of Hadacol Corner. It was unusually hot and dry that summer. The greasewood and mesquite that dominated the landscape had thick coatings of alkali. Not a day passed that a hot wind didn't launch what seemed like acres of the parched soil into the air and onto the crews' sunburned faces. Daylights turned out to be the least pleasant shift to work that summer, and, as usual, Whitey was not in the best of moods.

Their second well came in a fair producer, and the drilling crew began rigging down in preparation for skidding the rig to the next location. By mid-afternoon they had most of the subsidiary equipment moved and were ready to lower the derrick. The rig (which has since become the standard) was a relatively new innovation called a jackknife, so named because the derrick could fold down like a blade so that it would not have to be dismantled. All four legs of the derrick were secured at the base with metal pins. When two of the pins were removed, the traveling-block cables could actually lower the derrick to a horizontal position so it could be loaded on trucks in one piece and transported to a new location.

That particular afternoon it was Whitey's job as daylight driller to lower the derrick. He was skittish about the whole enterprise for two reasons. First he was still not as confident as he could be in the new technology, but mostly it was the unpredictable hot weather that had him on edge. Dust devils had whirled across the desolate landscape all afternoon, and Whitey feared that one might strike the operation at some critical moment. His tool pusher allowed that it didn't make much difference whether the wind blew or not because they had to have the rig skidded, rigged back up, and drilling without any delays.

Old Whitey did as he was told and sure enough there was hell to pay. As planned, the derrick started down slow and careful. Then, just as it reclined to a thirty-degree angle and the strain on the cables was at its greatest, along came one of those big old whirlwinds that Whitey had feared, headed right toward the derrick. As it moved across the rig, the derrick wobbled slightly to the left, then swung to the right and back left again. That was when the cables snapped and the whole apparatus collapsed atop a bit peddler's brand new Ford company car. Roughnecks ran around screaming and hollering; the bit man looked like he had seen a ghost; and Whitey leaned over to the tool pusher and said, "I told you so." Not to be outdone, the pusher called Whitey a sorry SOB and fired him on the spot. Whitey allowed that he couldn't be fired because he had quit the minute he saw that whirlwind heading their way. The pusher called him a damned liar, and they proceeded to wad up their fists and poke one another in the face.

By the time they finished, the dust had pretty much cleared, and the hands had calmed down somewhat. Later, as they all sat in the shade of the substructure eyeing the crumpled derrick lying across the new Ford's remains, another car came flying up in its own whirlwind. It was the drilling superintendent. It seems that losing a half-million-dollar rig upset him no end, so he fired the entire crew including the tool pusher. He also took it poorly that everybody was sitting in the shade sipping beer as they kibitzed about the carnage they had wrought.

That episode pretty much ended Whitey's oil-field career. He just couldn't seem to cope with all the changes that were going down in the patch. The last I heard of him he had opened a little beer joint on the edge of town where all his old cronies gathered on a regular basis to talk about the good old days and how things were going to hell with the younger generation in charge.

THE PROMOTER

Along about the end of World War I, Henry was operating out of Wichita Falls as an oil-well promoter. It is said that he floated so many oil-stock schemes that they had to put on an extra shift down at the Wichita County Courthouse just to keep up with the paper work he created. Sometimes he even resorted to hawking stock for nonexistent companies, but even for Henry that seemed a bit too risky. All that was past however when Henry hit upon his surefire scheme. He would promote investment in an oil well so far removed from proven producing grounds as to assure a dry hole. Selling high-priced shares in the well would guarantee him a tidy profit when the project failed, and some of his investors might even be induced to buy into another well.

It worked. Henry used the scheme time and again with unfailing success. Then the unthinkable happened. One of the wells came in a gusher. Investors appeared from everywhere clamoring for their share of the profits. It soon got out that the interests Henry had sold totaled 500 percent even though he claimed to maintain fifty-percent ownership. Naturally the conflict landed Henry in court.

When the case came to trial, dozens of investors testified how Henry had sold them ten-, twelve- or twenty-percent interests in the productive well. The promoter countered that they had simply misunderstood the deal. He was obviously raising capital for only one-half of the project, for he was reserving the other half for himself. The legal arguments raged

on for almost a week with Henry spending more than a day on the witness stand making an eloquent argument for his case. Eventually the jury retired to consider the evidence. It did not look good for Henry.

Shortly after the jury began its deliberations, Henry disappeared. Everybody went looking for him. Most assumed that he had slipped out ahead of a certainly unfavorable verdict. Finally, the bailiff happened to peek into the jury room, and there stood Henry. He was making a pitch to the jury on his next big oil project.

Collective memory is unclear as to the verdict ultimately rendered, but it's largely agreed that nine of the twelve men good and true put money in Henry's next well.

NITRO

The oil patch abounds with unforgettable characters. In bygone days the well shooter ranked high on that list, and for all I know, he might still be right up there. It takes an unusual personality to work with nitroglycerine on a daily basis. The steely nerves of those nitro handlers are legendary. No less legendary are some of the yarns of their personal exploits. One of those is recounted by John J. McLaurin in his book *Sketches in Crude Oil*, published in 1896.

It seems that a careless shooter somehow spilled a little liquid nitro on the floor of the magazine where it was stored. He did not notice it at the time, but later on when he happened to stomp down hard on his right heel he was immediately catapulted right up over the top of the derrick. Being a sure-footed devil, the shooter managed to land upright, but as soon as his left foot touched the ground, the same thing happened. Not wishing to repeat the ordeal, he removed his shoes, took a stiff shot of whisky to settle his nerves, and finished the job in his socks.

Though McLaurin doesn't mention it, that fellow might have been the same lonely well shooter who was so unpopular in his rooming house that he had to adopt a stray kitten for company. Admiring the kitten's feistiness, the shooter named him Nitro.

Unlike the other boarders, the kitten took to the shooter immediately, following him everywhere. They became so close that the shooter began to feed his pet small doses of nitroglycerine. Before long, little Nitro developed a real taste for the liquid explosive and wouldn't drink any milk that wasn't laced with it. Clearly, Nitro was developing a pretty serious problem, but like a lot of addicts, he did a fair job of hiding it. None of the other boarders knew about his habit.

That was unfortunate because not everyone in the house was a cat lover, least of all the grizzled old cable tool driller. He had absolutely no use for cats and no inclination to hide it. Every time little Nitro came near, he would break into cussing and throw whatever was at hand at the poor animal.

One day when the shooter was out in the field, the driller was just coming in off tour. As the driller opened the front door and stepped inside, Nitro made a mad dash for his freedom. The driller couldn't resist the opportunity to aim a mighty kick at the fleeing animal, but Nitro was too quick, and the momentum of failing to connect knocked the driller off his feet. At that the cat spun, hissed loudly, and spat at his tormentor. They say that the explosion was heard a mile away. Witnesses swore that last they saw the driller, whose boots were blown off, he was hightailing it barefoot, with old Nitro bounding behind, still hissing, and leaving small craters everywhere he spat.

20

THE DRILLER AND THE MONKEY

Oil-well drillers tell a host of stories on themselves. One of my favorites is the story of the driller and the monkey.

Some years ago a driller from West Texas took a job in South America. It paid extraordinarily well, but the location was deep in the Amazon jungle. What with the sweltering heat and everything else that went with working in a jungle climate, the driller had a devil of a time keeping good hands. Eventually, all the roughnecks from the states quit. He tried to replace them with men from the local labor pool, but they had no experience with heavy drilling machinery, and repair bills began to mount up.

In exasperation, the driller proclaimed to the tool pusher that he'd rather train a monkey from the surrounding jungle. One thing led to another, and soon it was a bet neither man could resist.

Before long the driller captured a strong healthy monkey who seemed to have a natural aptitude for roughnecking. Because of the monkey's climbing ability, the driller soon promoted him to derrick man. Within a couple of months the monkey was able to do almost every job on the rig. He became the best hand that driller had. Then one day the tool pusher showed up expecting to claim his winnings. Instead he was so impressed by what he saw that he fired the driller and gave his job to the monkey.

The humiliated driller could do nothing but go home in disgrace. He had not been back in West Texas more than a few months, however, when he received a letter from the Amazon. It was from the monkey who by then had replaced the tool pusher. He wanted the driller to come back down to South America and work for him.

THE ROUGHNECK'S TALE

I could tell he was an old timer from the patch the minute I laid eyes on him. Still solid and husky, he had the look of a man who had spent his life outdoors. His unruly gray hair could definitely have benefitted from shampoo and a comb. There was a chew of tobacco wedged between his cheek and a ragged row of stained teeth. His big gnarled hands were missing a couple of fingers but looked like they'd done enough work to outlast two or three bodies. He was leaning on the bar in the old Smoke House Pool Hall contemplating the Anheuser Busch picture on the wall while he sipped from a beer bottle gripped in his big right fist.

When I walked up and ordered my beer, he peered at me through bloodshot watery eyes, jerked his head toward the picture, and spoke.

"I was there," he said.

"You couldn't have been," I answered. "That's *Custer's Last Stand*."

He stared back at the image for a long minute before he answered. "Are you sure? I could swear that is a picture of Loffland Brothers rigging up."

At the time, my day job was gathering oral history interviews for a university archive, so I knew better than to let this one get away. I invited him to sit down and have another beer. By the time we had finished a six pack or so, I learned that he had roughnecked for just about everybody and had worked just about everywhere. It seems he got his start as a roughneck during the East Texas boom back in the '30s. Since then he had worked every patch between Louisiana and the West Coast. He even spent some time down in South America, and once took on a job in Africa that didn't work out too well.

But the damndest job ever was the time he hired out to "Curley" Simpson on a deep wildcat up in Alaska. He was never sure exactly who they were drilling for, but it didn't make much difference as long as the outfit paid regularly. He realized that something was strange about the job when he saw the derrick and realized how high it stood. It was not nearly so tall as the one that Gib Morgan and Big Toolie ran back in the early days—the one that had to be hinged in the middle to let the moon pass—but the one in Alaska was tall enough that they had to furnish the derrick man an oxygen mask. The rig was powered by twenty-four big Waukesha diesel engines that used so much fuel they had to build a two-inch line to the location just to keep them going. It was one big operation. Then he went on to relate his story.

"We spudded in on that well on a Monday. By the end of the week we were deeper than I had ever been before, and we just kept on drilling. It was so cold up there that steam froze up coming out of the boilers we used for heating the rig, and if you pitched your coffee out of a cup it froze to the ground in little upside down icicles. What with winter coming on and all and it being likely to get colder, most of the hands drug up and headed south to sunnier climes. That didn't seem to bother Curley a whole lot. He just replaced them with a crew of locals who had never operated anything more complicated than a dog sled. It got even worse by midwinter, and I thought we might have to shut down because that bunch of fur-clad boll weevils had damaged just about everything in the way of usable equipment on the location.

"By then the bottom hole temperature was so high that we had to run

in a heavy-duty heat-tempered drill bit and start using a specially con-cocted mud. Nobody was sure how deep we were when the blowout oc-curred. I was handling the mud pumps at the time and noticed that the pressure had dropped to nothing. It acted a lot like we had struck some sort of a big cavity. Almost immediately a scalding blast of steam shot out of the hole. Then molten lava began to flow out on the ground, con-gealing in the cold like thick molasses. Next thing we knew, the devil himself, complete with a forked tail, horns on his head, and a pitchfork in his hand, popped out of that hole. That's when the locals walked off.

"Old Satan was fit to be tied. The way he lit into Curley would have done any roughneck proud. The gist of it was that we had drilled clear down to hell where all that drilling mud was about to put his fires out, and he ordered Curley to put a stop to it. Curley was not having any of that from a pointy headed, red-faced civilian who couldn't keep his fires lit, even if he was the devil. He shot back in like fashion and then some, chastising the devil up one side and down the other for scaring off his crew and stopping work. If my recollection serves, they harangued one another for the better part of an hour while I tried to keep the mud pumps going. I guess those pumps were doing an excellent job, too. By the time those two ended their little tête-à-tête, I had the pressure headed back up, and that lava flow was dropping like a rock.

"The upshot was that the devil finally gave in and asked what it would take to get Curley to back off pumping drilling mud on his fires. The driller allowed that he had to finish the well on schedule, and being as how the devil had run off Curley's crew, it was up to him to find us a new one. They shook on the deal and in a little while old Nick showed back up with the crew he used to stoke his furnaces. That bunch in-cluded this ugly big-mouthed pirate fellow with dreadlocks for a beard, some sailor with a peg leg, and an assortment of other characters I took to be miscreants of one kind or another from the scars on their persons and the steel in their eyes. On average they were about what we were used to in a drilling crew.

"We put them to work right away before everything froze up, and in jig time we had that well cased off down through hell, which resolved the devil's problem. Then we went right back to drilling with that new crew of weevils. The work went on for another month and a half before we reached the formation Curley was looking for. By that time those fellows out of hell had made a fair bunch of roughnecks, except for the peg-leg who kept slipping on the drilling floor. We brought in that well flowing about 300 barrels per hour of the best hundred-proof vodka you ever laid a lip over. You might say I was surprised, but you couldn't say the same for Curley or the new crew. They didn't know any better, and Curley had evidently known all along.

"About a week after we completed the well and everybody had sobered up, Curley offered to keep that bunch of hands on for the next job instead of sending them back down to hell. To a man they turned him down because they all agreed that it was better to burn in hell than to work as a roughneck."

WHAT'S IN A NAME

Not many hands in the oil patch go by their given names. I doubt this has much to do with dubious pasts—after all, what could be more dubious than their present lifestyles? Nicknames just seem to be a hallmark of the trade. I never thought much about the guys I'd known only as "Blacky" or "Slim" or "Lefty" until I began gathering oral histories from the patch. Asking a coworker whether a particular roughneck might have been Henry Brown from Nacogdoches generally elicited a response such as, "You know, I worked with that fellow off and on for ten years and 'Lefty' was all I ever knew him by."

As much as this tended to thwart my research, it got me pondering the practice of nicknaming in the oil field. Sure some nicknames stemmed obviously from hair color, height, weight, or some other physical attribute. "Whiteys" and "Cottons" were cases in point. Take "Whitey" Harding for example. When I knew him in the 1950s, he was field man for the Maloney-Crawford Tank Company, but he had been around West Texas since the Santa Rita boom of the 1920s. Whitey's two light-complexioned sons were extremely freckle-faced. I worked with those boys off and on for twenty years and never knew them as anything but "Big Spec" and "Little Spec." I guess the Hardings' real first names will remain a mystery.

By accident I did discover the real first name of "Little Red" Michaels, another tank hand I worked with back then. Herman—but his wife was the only one who ever called him that. "Little Red" worked for years in a crew run by "Peewee" Johnson but eventually quit and went to work for "Beeky" Ezell over at Kermit. Other than the Harding boys, "Little Red" was the only hand I ever knew by a compound nickname.

Even if you escaped a nickname you might wind up with a qualifier. Take the McCameys, for example. George McCamey drilled the discovery well some miles west of the Santa Rita #1 near the present location of the town that was named for him. As it happened, there were three George McCameys working in West Texas in those days. The oil fraternity soon dubbed them as "Black" George, "Big" George, and "Lying" George. As to who was who, I have no idea because that was before my day. I knew them only by the stories that immortalized them.

Appellations deriving from weight never really set well with the roughnecks they were bestowed upon. "Fatso" and "Fatty" tended to provoke a swift challenge if you used it to a man's face. Less offensive and generally somewhat safer were "Jelly" and "Heavy." One who never seemed to mind was "Heavy" Brackeen, who came out of Oklahoma to Borger as a part-time cable tool driller and mostly full-time bootlegger. Later he moved his operation to Wink, but after a long and colorful career, "Heavy" settled into respectability and lived to enjoy a peaceful and comfortable old age.

Then there were those whose monikers were less common, like "Country" Glenn. He got his name playing football in high school. His coach had a hard time remembering names so he called Glenn "Country" and his brother "City" in order to differentiate between them. "Country" stayed with Glenn the rest of his life.

"Bo" Hobson used to be branch manager for the Union Tank Company in Odessa. He received his name from his own habit of addressing everybody else as Bo. When he asked, "How you doing, Bo?" you were never quite sure whether he couldn't quite place you or he was using it like *"Kid"* or "Bub."

Some of the more colorful oil-field monikers were fairly self-explanatory, like "Three Fingered" Jack Hilderbrand or "Dusty" Rhoades or "Steamboat" Fulton. But others like "Tap" Liddell or "Black Cat" Morgan were mystifying. If you were around long enough, you'd observe that "Checkbook" Myers earned the name from his habit of whipping out his checkbook to pay off a worker the moment he fired him.

I am not at all sure what "Haywire" Brown, "Ratchet-Mouth" Jones, or "Wide-Eyed" Yerkin might have to say about their monikers, but I am almost certain that even "Cry Baby" Hank Burks never complained too loudly so long as the checks didn't bounce.

THE TOUGHEST MAN IN OIL TOWN

Wide-Eyed Yerkin's specialty was acidizing wells. His tolerance for roiling fumes and intolerance for anything or one who got in his way had earned him a reputation. Among the tough crowd that caused most locals to lock away their money and daughters, Wide-Eyed was pretty much regarded as the roughest and rowdiest. One scorching August day out near Pyote in far West Texas, Wide-Eyed was finishing up, pumping the residue into an open pit. It was as hot as blue blazes—hell, it was hotter than Pecos—that day, and those chemicals put off such noxious fumes that even Wide-Eyed was forced to don an oxygen mask to get anywhere near the pit.

As he went about his work, he spotted a small dust cloud way off in the distance. After a bit the cloud grew closer, and he could make out a black dot beneath it. Eventually he could see a figure riding something bigger than a horse. When the entourage got close enough, there was the roughest-looking man he had ever seen. He was at least two heads taller than Wide-Eyed and had a good fifty pounds on him. The rider's long tangled beard couldn't conceal a jagged scar across his face. Wide-Eyed was beginning to think he needed more than an oxygen mask. He blinked hard, pulled away a corner of the mask, and spat. But when he looked up, no amount of blinking altered the apparition.

The rider was straddling a grizzly bear that he'd bridled with barbed wire. He spurred the beast unmercifully with a pair of *espuelas grandes* whose rowels were so large they'd have put conquistadors to shame. Whipping and hollering the whole way, he brandished a six-foot rattlesnake as a quirt.

As Wide-Eyed looked on in amazement, the rider reined the grizzly to a sliding halt and dismounted at a run. He bailed off into that acid pit and began to drink his fill. Then he removed his hat, dipped it full, dumped the liquid over his head, and sighed in contentment as it somewhat cooled his brow. Refreshed, the stranger strode out of the pit and started to remount.

Wide-Eyed managed to jerk out of his trance in time to utter, "Say friend, could I have a word—"

"Sorry," said the rider as he looked anxiously over his shoulder, "Nothing I'd like more than to stand here and jaw, but see that cloud over yonder? That's the toughest man in Oil Town, and he's closing in."

TAILING RODS

Those inside the oil fraternity know how much more there is to the patch than drilling oil wells. There are numerous other oil-field occupations, and wisely enough those engaged in them seldom venture outside their specialties. What the other fellow does may hardly be brain surgery, but there's always more to it than another might think. Hank, of course, had to find that out the hard way. One time work was so slow for "tanking" that Hank needed to make a few days at something else just to pay the bills. So he made the rounds of all the well-servicing outfits to see what he could pick up. Old Hank had never done any well servicing, but he figured that it couldn't be too hard a job considering the number of people he knew working at it. He finally caught one of the companies short handed, and they took him out on a job. It was a well swabbing operation, which looked to Hank for all the world like a bird's nest on the ground. It seemed that all these fellows did was lie around in the shade of the truck while the pulling machine did all the work. As the newest hand on the job, Hank had only to serve as lookout and awaken the crew in case the boss showed up. After a couple of days the well was clean enough that it began to flow, and they were done.

Then they sent him out on a rod-pulling job that was about half finished. Occasionally the sucker rods that pump oil wells have to be removed so the well can be repaired, and then the rods are replaced. In this particular situation the rods had already been removed and were ready to go back into the well. It didn't take Hank long to figure out why they were shorthanded.

The crew went out west of town a few miles to a sandy stretch of country where the land is so poor that nothing grows except little knee-high shinnery oak and a lot of grass burrs. The pulling unit was set up over the well, and neatly stacked to one side, on railroad ties, were about 5,000 feet of sucker rods in twenty-foot sections, ready to be returned to the well. The ties kept the rods out of the sand. The operator explained to Hank that he was to grab hold of the far end of the rod so that when the pulling unit began hoisting one end into the air the other would not drag in the sand. Hank was to keep his end out of the sand until he handed it off to one of the other workers who would fasten it to those already in the hole. Then the operator would lower the string of rods twenty feet, disconnect, pick up another rod, and repeat the operation until all of the rods were connected and back in the well. Hank's part of that operation was called tailing the rods. It sounded simple enough, and truly it was.

The first half dozen or so rods went as smooth as silk. Then the operator began to speed up. Before long the crew would have their connection made and a new rod hooked onto by the time Hank got back to his end. He had to trot to keep up. Once again the operator picked up his pace. Hank had to run to get hold of the next rod before the operator began to hoist. Running to catch hold was hard enough, but that blamed operator went just as fast moving the rod. Running through ankle-deep sand with a heavy sucker rod in your hand might be good training for some sort of Olympic event, but it didn't do much for Hank's disposition. Nor did it help that the operator kept hollering and cussing for the rod tailer to hurry up.

By the time they stopped for lunch, Hank was a sight from being dragged through the sand on the ends of those heavy rods. His overalls were torn in two or three places, and he had stickers just about everywhere in his hide. He was so tired he could hardly stand, and that big pile of rods was only about half gone. Hank must have run at least ten or twelve miles through sand by then. While they were eating, the operator declared that they hadn't got much done that morning, but the crew would sure give it hell that afternoon.

With that Hank gathered up his street clothes, flagged down a passing Halliburton truck, and rode back to town. He didn't even go back to pick up his check. Our hero just chalked the episode up to experience and vowed he'd learned his lesson. Easy money in the oil field is seldom what it seems.

SO YOU WANT TO BUILD A MUSEUM EXHIBIT
Or, Bringing the Oil Patch to a Higher Cultural Level

Most museums regardless of their mandate share certain commonalities. They are largely dependent upon the generosity of wealthy patrons (usually too few), hire staffs with specific academic specialties (not necessarily adequate to the task), and fulfill their missions through the medium of exhibitions (never sufficiently funded and always beset with obstacles that no one anticipates). The new petroleum wing I oversaw in my Panhandle days is a case in point. For all my hard-won diplomas, I might as well have been back in the patch.

A grand dame had donated a ton of money to build the wing. Her late husband had been a preeminent oilman, so she stipulated that the space be dedicated to a petroleum-related exhibit. Because I was the only person on staff who knew the difference between a roughneck and a roustabout, I drew the short straw. Suddenly I was in charge. Not that I was ungrateful.

I could well envision an ambitious undertaking that drew upon knowledge of long-gone technology and just the right grasp of regional history to interpret the story properly. The central object in the wing was to be a full-sized cable-tool drilling rig of wood construction and was to fill the wing's eighty-six-foot wide and forty-two-foot high glass-enclosed foyer. All I had to do was figure out how to erect the monstrosity. But with the help of a couple of 1920s oilfield equipment catalogs and two or three oral history interviews with old-timers from the patch, I was getting a pretty clear picture of what to do. Unfortunately, leaving in the dark of the night was not an option.

All in all, we developed a respectable plan for the installation except for one minor flaw. In the interest of authenticity, the plan called for period equipment to construct the rig and then become part of the actual exhibit. It was a stroke of curatorial genius—unfortunately just not one we'd budgeted for. Determined to rectify that oversight, I gathered up a case or two of cold beer (strictly for lubrication purposes) and set out around the oil patch to acquire said working artifacts. Some accessions required more beer than others, but I'd managed to get title to all the necessary items when it occurred to me that the means for moving those multi-thousand-pound objects presented no small difficulty or cost. As generous as the grand dame's donation had been, such expenses were just not in the budget. Museums are designated nonprofit for a very good reason; the necessary additional funds were sorely lacking.

Nevertheless, with the help of Anheuser Busch (that is, my good friends Bud and Bud Lite) and some creative con artistry, we soon managed to transport a massive pile of timbers and assorted heavy steel objects that with a little modification would soon pass for artifacts.

About that time it occurred to me that the rig, once constructed, might be too heavy for the floor to support so I consulted a couple of engineers on the subject. They allowed that it could be done if the weight was distributed just right and providing, of course, that my weight estimates were accurate. Then, as an afterthought, they mentioned that the structure had to set at least three feet back from those massive glass windows unless I enjoyed watching them pop out of their framework like corks out of a bottle. With that technical information firmly in hand and the sure knowledge that my best guess on weight was probably correct within a margin of plus or minus eighty to ninety percent we set to work.

Progress on the exhibit proceeded reasonably fast considering that donor's desire for involvement, the inadequacies of our antiquated equipment, and our building crew who were, well, essentially a bunch of boll weevils on a nonprofit payroll. Otherwise we hardly hit a snag—except for the band-wheel incident. For those not conversant with early day oil-field equipment, a band wheel is wooden, but it's ten feet in diameter and one foot thick with a steel shaft through its center to which is attached a variety of metal accouterments. All in all, it weighs a smidgeon over 5,000 pounds. With my usual dead-on faculty for estimation, I had her nailed at 3,000.

Using the full power of our trusty no-account forklift (donated by a patron who got a hefty tax writeoff for his trouble), we maneuvered that wheel through the narrow opening into the exhibition area without destroying anything of significance. Although the floor got a little shaky from time to time, nothing collapsed so I figured we were doing just fine. Then to raise the wheel into place we used a big old logging chain, attaching one end to the wheel and wrapping the other around the forks of the lift.

But it wasn't till our first attempt to lift the wheel that 3,000 pounds seemed a little on the low side. The back wheels of the forklift came off the floor. We moved the chains a little closer to the lift and tried again. The forklift was steadier, but still a little light in the behind. So we sat a couple of janitors who didn't seem otherwise occupied on the back of the lift to give us more counterweight. That did the trick. We raised that band wheel about six inches off the floor and began to ease forward when it happened. Unbeknownst to us, someone had replaced one link of that chain with one of those temporary ones you buy down at the hardware store for about fifty cents, and it did about what you would expect. When that band wheel hit the floor, dust flew everywhere; those big glass windows shook and quivered like Jell-O; and a double-fist-sized divot marred the delicate aesthetic of the dyed concrete floor. On the positive side, however, the wheel must have struck the floor right over a reinforcement beam because, once again, nothing collapsed.

As luck would have it the museum's executive director had happened by and witnessed the entire incident. He looked me straight in the eye and said something on the order of WHAT were you thinking! That was his mistake. I was standing there in that hot foyer with my nerves twitching like the end of the broken logging chain and sweat was pouring off me onto that dyed concrete. Our counterweights, having been bucked off the forklift like off a bronc, were lying on the floor whining something about workman's comp, and the lift driver was slumped over the steering wheel whitefaced and motionless. The only thing moving was Billy, the carpenter, who was cussing a blue streak. When I grabbed for Billy's claw hammer, the director ducked out of range, which probably saved all of us a lot of unnecessary grief.

At any rate the petroleum wing was finally completed. We had a giant reception where the director praised all involved in the undertaking. The grand dame was pleased with the result and said so. In that glass foyer, the rig still awes the public with its magnificence and beckons them to what continues to be a pretty impressive short course in regional history. But I doubt that any of them knows just how much a story of the patch that petroleum wing truly is.

Two
RIDING THE RANGE

Nothing associated with Texas folk life has received more attention than ranching and its legendary hero, the cowboy. From the dime novel to the multimillion–dollar screen, nothing has loomed larger in Texas lore. Although most Texans are proud to lay claim to the mythology that Hollywood perpetuates, even though realism and historical accuracy become blurred in western film, a diminishing few know firsthand the life and lot of those whose job, at the end of the day, is still to feed and water the livestock.

For me, the lynch pin of Texas mythology lies not so much in what is larger than life but in the smaller quirkiness that serves day to day to define the cowboy spirit, that streak of independence that may turn a cowboy's investment strategy to racehorses instead of IRAs or grain futures, that brand of entrepreneurship that recognizes in the need for dead animal disposal, the opportunity for a business named Your Local Used Cow Company. These for me are the sort of elements that have informed the best of a living lore since the days of the great trail drives.

THE GATE

Anyone who knows ranching knows that its first law is that you always shut the gate. No matter what the circumstance, when you open a gate to a pasture and drive through it, you close it behind you. Over the years this has caused many an argument as to who drives the pickup and who rides shotgun, as it's the latter's lot to climb out and get the gate. Though ranch hands may grumble, or even fight, over who gets the honor of riding shotgun, it's generally outsiders who forget or outright ignore the cardinal rule of the gate.

A few years back one tough old foreman who'd been cowboying since he could walk became so aggravated by a repeat offender that he began to lie in wait for the culprit. It took almost a week, which did nothing for his disposition, but he caught the rascal in the act. Just as the foreman suspected, it was a truck driver for the oil company operating some leases on the ranch. The rancher cut off the burly driver as he began to drive away from the gate he had left open.

After much jawing back and forth the driver allowed that he did not have time to close the damned gate or waste any more time arguing about it. The rancher did not quite see it that way, and the confrontation escalated. The resulting fist fight covered a lot of ground and went on for the better part of an afternoon. They tore up brush all over that end of the pasture. Some said that they raised a dust cloud that could be seen for a mile or more. Sometimes one got the better, and sometimes the other prevailed. Ultimately the truck driver carried the day. As he climbed back into his vehicle and drove away, the rancher waved to him and declared, "Never mind. I'll get the gate."

Eventually the matter landed in court, where the judge asked the rancher just exactly what the fight was over. "Close as I can recall, Your Honor," the rancher replied, "nearly a quarter of a section."

SOAP AND WATER

Roundup cooks have a well-earned reputation for being cantankerous. A good one is always hard to find and harder to keep. Nobody wants to cross him once he is on the job. This is amply illustrated by the cowboy who complained that there was too much baking powder in the biscuits. When he glanced up and saw the cook glaring at him he quickly added, "Sure makes 'em tasty." In the full flush of roundup, only a fool would jeopardize the grub supply line.

As long as anybody could remember, Limpy had rustled grub for one outfit or another out in the sandhill country southeast of Monahans. Some said that he had earned his name as a bronc peeler back in his younger days when he was bucked off so many times that he couldn't walk right. After that he made the jump from top hand to cook. Interestingly enough, he made a pretty good cook whose Dutch-oven repertoire included an outstanding cobbler. If he had a drawback, other than being about the most contrary human alive, it was his total disregard for personal hygiene. The man simply had a strong aversion to bathing. When cowboys notice, that's a serious indictment.

Probably the only real friends Limpy had were a pair of scarred-up old greyhounds that he called Soap and Water. They accompanied him everywhere. As it turned out Limpy was an avid coyote hunter who used the dogs to catch his quarry. When they were not out chasing coyotes, the critters usually lolled around in the shade beneath the chuck wagon enjoying scraps from the meals Limpy cooked. And woe betide the luckless cowboy who kicked those dogs or made any other overt move against the animals for they served another useful purpose.

Despite Limpy's well-known resistance to sanitation, all his pots, pans, and other cooking utensils were spotless thanks to the unrelenting efforts of old Soap and Water in their spare time beneath the wagon.

THE WASH PAN

Way back before the country settled up, Old Man McWhorter ranched out in West Texas in what would later become Gaines County. His place was so isolated that he managed to get into town only once or twice a year. Luxuries on the ranch were few and usually depended on his annual trip to Kansas City to sell his beef. Just before he left one year he inquired of the Missus what he could bring her from the big city. The only thing she could think of was a big graniteware basin so the hands could wash up before entering the house for supper.

When he got to Kansas City the old man searched out three or four big hardware stores before he found exactly what he wanted. It was a glorious wash basin. Three feet across and sporting a mottled-blue enamel finish in the latest fashion, it was sure to please Mrs. McWhorter.

When the rancher arrived back home, he drove a big old sixteen-penny nail into one of the windmill legs and hung the new pan there by a hole in its rim. There it stayed. As the rancher had hoped, it was Mrs. McWhorter's pride. Better yet it got a lot of use from the cowboys, especially come spring when the winds and dirt picked up, as they will in West Texas. One day it came an unusually strong wind. Though it started as just a breeze, it soon approached gale-force speed, and that dish pan began to whirl around on the nail. The higher the wind grew, the faster the pan revolved until finally it came loose and began to roll across the prairie. The farther it rolled, the faster it went until before you knew it, the thing was almost out of sight.

Old Man McWhorter, who happened to be watching when the pan came loose, was devastated to see such a valuable piece of ranch property taking off. Quick as lightning he saddled up his best horse and headed out in hot pursuit. At first he whipped and spurred like all get out, but it was soon apparent there was no hope of overtaking his quarry. So he settled into a steady pace, following the basin's trail for ten miles or more before the wind died down enough that he could catch up.

It was along about dusk when the rancher made it back to the ranch house, the prize tied firmly to his saddle horn. But wouldn't you know it, that big beautiful thirty-six-inch-wide pride of the ranch had worn down to a three-quart sauce pan.

FIREWOOD

Back when homesteaders first settled up the West Texas ranch country, a natural animosity between newly arrived farmers and long-established ranchers played out in many ways and sometimes with unexpected results. Take, for example, the situation that developed over the question of ownership rights to the dead timber from the river bottom—the primary source of firewood in a largely treeless land.

It happened that a homesteader took his wagon down into the river bottoms along the Salt Fork of the Brazos to gather a load of firewood. He arrived just at the break of day, and it was well after noon before he finished piling his wagon high with deadwood that had accumulated. Just as he completed his task, three cowboys who worked for one of the big spreads in the area rode up. They looked the situation over and decided to teach the farmer a lesson he would not soon forget.

The cowboys allowed as to how the fallen timber belonged to the ranch and the farmer could not have it. The nester argued that he had as much right to the wood as anybody and the cowboys should best be on their way. The argument waxed hot and heavy for a while until finally one of the cowboys abruptly stated that the farmer had better unload the wood if he knew what was best for him. Outnumbered as he was, the farmer saw the futility of his situation and set to work throwing the wood out of his wagon.

It took a while, but the man finally tossed the last log onto the ground to the delight of the watching cowboys. Then he picked up his shotgun that had been lying in the wagon bed beneath the wood and said, "All right, boys, you can fill her back up now."

THE LEGEND OF BLACK QUESTION

Black Question was a bull. Not just any bull, but one of those big old bucking Brahmas you see on the rodeo circuit. From a distance he didn't look so tough, but up close that critter was downright scary. He was coal black from stem to stern except for one little white patch shaped like a question mark right in the middle of his forehead. He raised bucking off rodeo would-be's to a fine art.

Jim was not much of a rodeo hand, but like so many young men out in West Texas he loved the sport. Some say that rodeo is all about the need for man to gain dominion over beast. Others maintain that it is about competitive challenge and personal bests. Just the same, in the case of most young men competing, I'm pretty sure that the lovely young women flocking to the arena and the dances afterward have as much to do with it as anything. Such was certainly the case with Jim, who would occasionally climb on something with four legs that could buck, but he was not particularly keen on bull riding. It probably had something to do with the concussion he got that time down at Big Lake.

Jim and Black Question got acquainted at the junior rodeo at Big Spring one memorable spring night. Because none of us could afford a good horse for steer roping, a number of us decided to enter the bull-riding competition, but Jim came along only for the dance. He hadn't planned to enter any of the events. As the evening progressed, however, we managed to get him sufficiently inebriated to agree to enter the bull-riding contest along with the rest of us. As misfortune would have it, he drew Black Question for his ride.

We all went out to the stock pens behind the arena to check out our respective mounts. When Jim saw that big black bull, you could see the blood drain from his face. I thought for a minute he was going to back out, but after a couple more beers his color returned, and he regained what little confidence he once had. The die was cast, and before long the show began.

I don't know whether it was good bucking stock or bad karma that night, but every bull rider in the contest was getting thrown before the whistle blew. Finally, it came time for Jim to come out on Black Question. He borrowed my bull rope, used about a ton of rosin on his riding glove, and took a firm grip. The boy was scared to death. That bull left the chute bucking. He jumped and spun and did everything I ever saw a bull do to throw a rider. But old Jim just sat up there like a tick on a dog and rode that bull till the whistle blew. He was the only one of us who finished in the money.

Jim never mounted another head of rough stock after that night. The truth of the matter is that he got his riding hand hung up in that bull rope and for the first time in his life he was forced to finish a ride. That accomplished all he ever desired in the way of rodeoing. Nonetheless, for years afterward, he remained a fixture at rodeo dances, where he was revered as the man who rode Black Question. As for that bad Brahma bull, he became famous as the only rodeo bull ridden only once in his entire bucking career.

THE BULLFIGHTER

Heroes are sometimes bred on the most unlikely proving grounds. Such was the case with Frank, who enrolled with a group of his buddies down at Sul Ross University the fall after they finished high school. It was not so much an education that they wanted as to join the crackerjack rodeo team. In Alpine they rented a little two-bedroom house that soon became cluttered with saddles and bridles and roping cans and a variety of other rodeo accouterments. As they made rodeos all over the country, their grades suffered in proportion to the time they spent on the circuit.

Given their proximity to Mexico, Frank soon became well known in the bars of the border towns for an unusual talent. He owned a unicycle that he never traveled without. I doubt that he ever paid for a drink so long as he had that single-wheeled marvel. Whenever Frank mounted that cycle a crowd would gather. He would ride it into a bar, and the crowd would follow right along. Bartenders were quick to keep him in free drinks, and the more alcohol he consumed, the more daring the tricks he performed. There is no telling how many chairs were broken or how many drinks were spilled on account of that unicycle. It was a sight to behold.

Then came the day that Frank and his buddies decided to take in a local bullfight. They'd put in a good amount of time in the bars the day before, and by the time they got to the bullring, they were feeling fairly

bulletproof. When the bullfight began it soon became obvious that only second-rate matadors plied their trade in the small border town. In a word, it was dull, and the crowd grew restive. In a pique, Frank whipped off his denim jacket, and with jacket in one hand and beer bottle in the other he vaulted into the arena. That bull made a pass at the would-be matador, who managed to divert his attacker with the jacket before delivering a coup de grace over the head with a half-full bottle of beer. The crowd went wild, and Frank grinned from ear to ear as he bowed to all and sundry.

Seizing the moment, the guys handed over the unicycle and another *cervesa,* which Frank began to guzzle as he pedaled around the ring. The bull, somewhat taken aback, stood rooted in the center of the ring, as the crowd went crazy. Frank was in his element. Shouting *"Toro, Toro,"* he pedaled up to the bull and slapped him in the face with that denim jacket. Snapping out of his reverie, the bull charged, whereupon Frank did a quick reverse pedal and cracked him over the head again. By this time the spectators were throwing stuff into the ring and screaming *"Olé"* at the top of their lungs. That was when Frank decided to take a victory lap around the ring, waving his jacket at the crowd and dodging various officials who hoped to eject him from the premises. In the excitement everybody forgot about the bull. I'm pretty sure Frank heard him coming because he turned his head just before old *Toro* ripped into that unicycle. Now I've been to lots of rodeos and seen any number of cowboys thrown, but I've never seen anybody go quite so high as Frank did that day down in Mexico. He soared like a bird and came down in the third row of seats.

Luckily he wasn't hurt too badly. The Mexican doctor who patched him up said that a broken arm and a slight concussion were a small price to pay for the rejuvenation of bullfighting on the border. A local promoter offered Frank a contract to reenact his performance every other Sunday for the rest of the season. But once he sobered up, Frank decided it was wiser to go out on top.

To this day, if you pay attention in those small border towns, you can still hear *corridas* sung in honor of the gringo matador who miraculously appeared that memorable Sunday and then just as mysteriously disappeared.

THE WOLF HUNTER

Rex McQueen was a cowboy all his life. When I knew him, he was managing old Sid Kyle's place up north of Orla on the New Mexico line. Rex was one of those men trying desperately to stave off civilization, which seemed to be threatening his way of life. That was probably why he never allowed a telephone to be installed at the house and seldom ventured off the ranch. He did enjoy the advantages of electricity, probably because Polly insisted on it and besides from time to time the cowboy enjoyed a good baseball game on an ancient rabbit-eared television in the living room.

Besides Polly, Rex had two other passions in life. Working cattle—at one memorable branding he roped 128 calves without a single miss—and wolf hunting.

So okay, there weren't really any wolves in West Texas then, only coyotes, but Rex and his cohorts called them wolves anyway. In those days my dad would take his pack of hounds out to the ranch where he would pair them with Rex's pack. They spent weeks at a time out there tending cattle by day and listening to the chase by night. Eventually Rex sold his pack of hounds and in their stead purchased two rawboned greyhounds that he dubbed Gabe and Walker after a popular television commercial of the day. It took a while, but eventually he trained those dogs to chase coyotes. Most hounds hunt by scent, but greyhounds hunt mostly by sight, which tends to make theirs a daytime sport.

At first Gabe and Walker chased coyotes together, but they soon discovered that superior speed was no advantage over the coyotes' staying power. If the quarry survived the greyhounds' initial burst of speed, then more often than not it escaped unharmed after a long and difficult chase.

But those dogs were smart. Once they realized that coyotes run in long circular patterns covering several miles, Gabe and Walker changed their tactics. When they jumped a coyote, only one would give chase. The other would remain at the starting point. When the coyote completed his circuit, the rested dog would take up the pursuit, and his compatriot would rest. By working shifts on the coyote, the greyhounds nearly always exhausted their quarry and caught him.

The show Gabe and Walker put on was amazing to behold. As Rex tooled around the ranch in his pickup, the dogs would stand in the bed alertly eyeing the landscape. When they spotted a coyote, they would both bail out of that truck no matter its speed, and the chase was on. Then they would work their magic and before long another ranch pest was eradicated.

Rex kept old Gabe and Walker even after they were so old and stove up that they couldn't hunt anymore. He went back to his night hunting with my dad and other wolf-hunting buddies but never bought another pair of greyhounds. I suppose he never believed he could find their equal. Gabe and Walker have long since gone to their reward, as has Rex, but the memory of those wolf hunts lingers on in that barren Loving County country up on the New Mexico line.

Three
DOWN ON THE FARM

West Texas came to agriculture late. Though ranchers began claiming that semiarid land in the late nineteenth century, it was not until the early twentieth that farmers sought to tame it. Scant rainfall, however, discouraged all but the hardy—or optimistic—from remaining. What else do you call anyone who can lose crop after crop to drought and continue to believe that next year it is sure to rain?

And who's to say that Mother Nature, especially in West Texas, hasn't answered farmers' prayers for water in unexpected ways? Take the case of the farmer who spent most of the spring and summer digging a well only to have it come up dry. Just as he was about to give up any hope of a groundwater supply, a tornado came along, sucked that well right out of the ground, and smashed it down again about a quarter of a mile away. That new location gushed water with such force that the farmer was able to irrigate more than 200 acres of prime cotton land.

Such miraculous good fortune was hardly commonplace, but adventures in West Texas farming have produced some interesting tales.

THE CROP DUSTER

I met him on the Texas Tech campus in the summer of '69. He was
an athletic young fellow in his mid-twenties who wore expensive clothes,
sported aviator's sunglasses, and drove a bright red Corvette newly off
the showroom floor. At first I mistook him for a slightly over-age frat rat,
but his demeanor was flashier and hard edged. So I guessed that he
might be one of those jet jockeys from out at Reese Air Force Base. I was
almost right.

Once we got better acquainted, I learned that he was a grounded crop
duster. The authorities had pulled his flying license after a slight
mishap—actually, he eventually fessed up, after a series of mishaps. It
was unlikely that he would get off the ground in the foreseeable future.
Given that dismal prospect he'd decided that he might as well go to college seeing as how he had plenty of money and nothing else particularly
pressing in his life.

That summer he told me a lot about crop-dusting. It seems he usually
worked early in the mornings when the wind was still and the insecticide
cloud would float directly down on the crop, without any drift, so as not
to endanger any nearby chickens or other small livestock. To get good
coverage, he always flew as low as possible, or sometimes lower—which
seems by and large to have been the source of his troubles.

Once when he was dusting a cotton crop a little south of Lubbock, he
had to fly toward a power line that was too low to pass beneath. Thus, as
he approached the end of his pass he had to execute a steep climb and

bank hard right, back to the beginning of his run. On the far side of the power line, and running parallel to it, was a railroad track, and between the track and the line lay one of those little county roads.

Making that climb and turn was a particularly tedious maneuver that required fine coordination and a steady hand. On this particular day the first five passes went fine. Then on the sixth run he miscalculated slightly and had to throttle wide open into an almost vertical climb. Just at the apex of that climb, the propeller came right off that airplane. Our hero somehow managed to nose the craft over before it stalled out. Then he banked hard right to bring the craft in attitude to land on that little country lane. All in all, it was an admirable demonstration of flying expertise.

About that time he spotted a pickup truck traveling down the lane in the same direction he had chosen. By then he had cut the engine so the truck driver was unaware of his approach. Once again the skillful pilot remained in control of the situation as he managed his air speed to land directly behind the truck. In all likelihood, he might even have come to stop without over-running the pickup—if only one of the farm laborers riding in the bed hadn't looked up and seen him coming. When the terrified laborer commenced beating on the pickup cab with his fist, the driver threw on his brakes, and all hell broke loose. The doors of that truck flew open and disgorged its occupants while the hands in the back dived into the bar ditches on either side of the road. The plane's wheels bounced off the top of the pickup cab causing the craft to careen from its carefully planned trajectory. By the time the dust settled, one wing of the plane was crumpled, a bunch of itinerant workers had a story that no one back home would likely believe, and the duster had a lump on his head to match the size of the blot on his flying record.

Of the intrepid duster's other misfortunes, I remember best the one that finally bound him to earth. It happened out west of Slaton early one summer morning when he was spraying a big field of sorghum.

This time there were no power lines or trees or other serious obstacles that would seem to require extraordinary feats or maneuvers. There was, however, a telephone line strung along the top of a fence that ran a mile or so from the farm-to-market road bordering one side of the field to a farmhouse. It stuck up about five feet and all the pilot had to do was clear it as he began his pass. Everything worked just fine and dandy through about half the job until a slight wobble caused one rear wheel of the plane to snag the phone line. The duster knew instantly what had happened and gunned the engine, hoping that he would either break the line or tear the wheel off. The more power he applied, the more phone line he tore loose, and the more altitude he lost. Before long he was trailing a half-mile of that wire, and his prop was heading sorghum like some monstrous threshing machine. Then the plane nosed in, and the pilot went through her windshield like a bullet.

Witnesses rushed to a nearby farmhouse (one whose phone service had not been interrupted) and called into Slaton for help. The pilot lay out in that hot sorghum all bloodied and broken, waiting for rescuers to race the five miles from town to the scene of the accident. Yet an hour later it was not paramedics who arrived, but an undertaker, in a hearse. It seemed the undertaker also owned the ambulance service, but convinced the duster had to be dead, saw no point in hurrying or bringing the ambulance. With that the semiconscious pilot summoned the strength to rise to his feet, issue a few choice epithets, and knock that undertaker cold. Then the duster fainted dead away.

I never heard whether he went back to dusting. But one thing was plain. He was probably a lot better pilot and yarn spinner than he was a student because he failed the course we were taking that summer.

THE COTTON PATCH

Uncle "Preach" moved out to farming country along the Prairie Dog Town Fork of the Red River north of Quitaque along about the end of World War II. He had spent his life raising cotton back in Central Texas and thought he knew everything there was to know about the crop. But things were different out west, and he had to retrain in a hurry.

The biggest differences were irrigation and the expanse of the fields. Back home nobody irrigated because it rained a lot, usually too much. Of course you didn't have to irrigate in West Texas, either, he learned. You could always dry-land farm—if you were content to make a decent crop every five or six years. Equally dismaying was the acreage it took to farm cotton in West Texas. In comparison to the sixty- to eighty-acre patches he was accustomed to farming, those several-hundred-acre fields seemed enormous. Luckily Uncle Preach was a quick study, and things worked out for the best.

Nevertheless, when he traveled downstate to visit friends and relatives, Uncle Preach loved nothing better than holding forth on how different life was out west. Of course any repertoire can stand freshening over time, and as Uncle Preach's material became too familiar, he had to work to keep West Texas as grand as his listeners' expectations of the vast landscape Uncle Preach now called home.

And that may explain how he came to tell us about his scheme with a promoter named Jake. It seems that Jake had heard about Uncle

Preach's prowess as a cotton grower and was looking for a partner. Jake had put together a block of land up on the High Plains that measured a bit more than 2,000 sections or upwards of a million and a quarter acres and wanted to plant it all in cotton. The prospect intrigued Uncle Preach, and they soon struck a bargain.

The rows in that cotton patch ran straight for eighty-seven miles from north to south to take advantage of the slope of the land. Preach and Jake drilled 2,500 irrigation wells up on the north end, and it took fifteen days for the water to run all the way south. Even at a fast clip, it took a full twenty-four hours for a tractor pulling a planter to make a round. But because the long run was so straight, they were able to rig the tractors to run without drivers, which amounted to a great savings in labor. All in all, it still looked like a money-making proposition.

They pumped so much water that first year that the aquifer dropped a full twelve feet. By fall it looked like they would make a bumper crop, even though 3,000 acres were hailed out and another 2,000 blown out. To pick the crop they had to bring in 10,000 *braceros*. It took one man a week to pick one row, and he had to replace his worn-out cotton sack at the end. Even so, those hands were picking 9,000 bales a day, and everything looked good.

Unfortunately, Preach and Jake's foresight hadn't extended to the ginning process. They'd overlooked the fact that there were only enough gins in the area to process about a thousand or so bales per day. That meant that most of the crop had to be stored where it was picked. To make matters worse, unusually heavy rains fell, ruining most of what was left in the field right where it lay. Just when things seemed bleakest, however, the bankers came through in true fashion and financed a string of new cotton gins.

Come planting season, Preach and Jake started up again in high spirits, and things went great if you discount those few runaway tractors that caused a major collision or two out on the highway. Then the wells began to run dry. By the fourth of July, they were out of water, and by harvest time, all that was left of the crop were miles and miles of dried-up stalks. The bankers foreclosed; the fields disappeared in a haze of blowing dirt; and Jake took out for parts unknown.

Uncle Preach always ended by saying the experience pretty much summed up farming in West Texas. If the weather doesn't get you, the bankers will.

HAULING HOGS

Future Farmers of America has done as much as anything to nurture young agribusinessmen in West Texas. And the year Curt chose swine-raising as his project, he did the Odessa chapter proud. His first feat was securing four well-bred pigs to feed out down at the FFA barns. After months of grooming, walking, and carefully adjusting feed for maximum growth and sheen, Curt was pleased to see his hogs top out at 200 pounds by the time of the Sandhills Hereford and Quarter Horse Show, where they took several prizes. When Curt was subsequently invited to show two pigs at the Houston fat stock show, he displayed considerable business sense by selecting the best one of his original four, then purchasing an equally fine eligible hog from a classmate who could not make the trip. In Houston, Curt's hog placed second in its class, and the one he bought placed first in a brand-new category, mostly because he was one of only three entered. But that didn't diminish Curt's euphoria. He knew he'd found his calling.

As soon as he graduated from high school, the budding hog farmer went into partnership with the FFA teacher and began raising pigs. They got some pens out near the edge of town, contracted with the school cafeterias for their garbage, and were soon feeding out about a hundred young swine. Slopping a hundred hungry hogs each day proved interesting work, particularly in wet weather when the mud got deep and the garbage began to smell. Even as his social life struck a downhill course

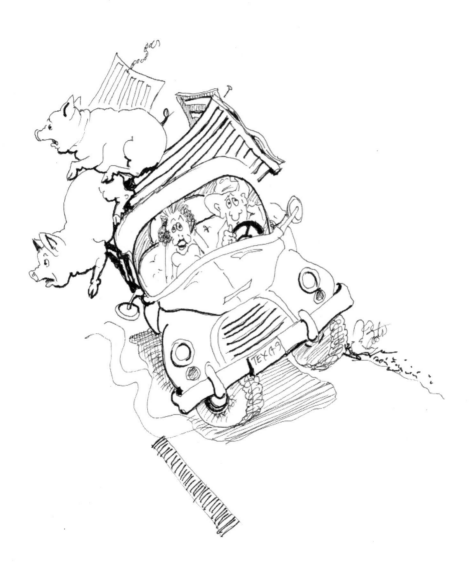

that no combination of Lifebuoy, Right Guard, and Old Spice seemed able to reverse, Curt persisted.

Finally, as it approached time to take the hogs to market, Curt decided to test the waters at a livestock sale at Lamesa. Accordingly, he outfitted his pickup with a hitch, borrowed a stock trailer from a friend, loaded a half dozen of his best stock, and set out for the sale.

Now hauling hogs is a somewhat different proposition than transporting other livestock, largely owing to porcine physique. Short legs and rotund profiles just don't make for superb balance. Those with experience in the hog business report that unless they're packed in like sardines, swine have a tendency to slip about or fall down, thereby shifting a trailer's center of gravity. This is particularly a problem in the event of sudden stops or sharp turns. If Curt's older and wiser partner had warned him about all this, Curt had either not heard or was just too young to care.

On the morning of the sale, Curt headed off in a cloud of dust with the stock trailer about half full of well-fed hogs. As his spirits soared, so did the speedometer needle, reaching well beyond seventy miles per hour. Not wanting to be delayed by a slow-moving pickup just ahead of him, Curt whipped over to pass it with a flourish. When he pulled back into his lane, however, the trailer didn't. That was probably because all those hogs were stacked like cord wood on the side where they had fallen. As Curt maneuvered to correct his error, the hogs struggled to right themselves, swinging the trailer sharply in the opposite direction, which of course toppled the hogs to the other side.

In desperation, Curt tried braking, which brought the careening trailer right up alongside the cab, so close that he could look directly into the face of a squealing pig. Curt wasn't squealing, but he was definitely more terrified than the pig.

In the contest of wills between the half-loaded trailer and the pickup, the latter was clearly the loser, pitching so far over on one side and then the other that it scraped the pavement each way, sending up streams of sparks and wreaking unspeakable damage on the suspension.

There's no telling what would have happened if that trailer hitch had not broken, which I'm sure is all that saved the pickup from overturning. Of course it didn't do much for that load of hogs. They sailed over a barbed wire fence and out across the pasture in a massive cloud of dust. Miraculously, none of them were killed, but they scattered so far that it would take the rest of the day to round them up. By the time Curt brought his truck under control and to a stop, the slow-moving pickup he had passed had caught up and pulled in behind him. Its driver, an old farmer, sauntered up, saw that Curt was all right, and observed, "Ain't never hauled no hogs before, have you boy?"

Shortly afterward Curt sold his share of the operation at a loss, burned his hog-farming clothes, joined the army, and shipped out to Vietnam. Fortunately, he met with no experience there as harrowing as his trip to the sale barn, and Curt never regretted leaving the hog business.

Four
WEATHER

West Texas, like most Plains country west of the hundredth meridian, is indisputably semiarid. That means its residents can count on hot and dry. They can also count on less annual rainfall than the twenty inches considered minimal for normal agriculture. What they can't count on is when or how that rain, always capricious, will fall. This is amply illustrated by the tale of the newcomer who marveled to a local farmer how little it rained here. "Well," the farmer replied, "it sure seemed like a lot the day it fell."

On the other hand, nothing in West Texas is more predictable than the wind. It always blows. Sometimes it really blows. In spring and fall it can suck tons of loose soil up into infamous sandstorms that can darken the sky day after day. Employing their ever distinctive brand of humor, West Texans have learned, of course, to take it all in stride—like the old cowboy who claimed not to pay sandstorms much mind unless he could see wagon tracks in the sky.

In spring and summer West Texas heat can generate dramatic thunderstorms whose lightning bolts fill the sky with spectacular displays that sometimes reveal a tornado dancing across the landscape. But it is not always sandstorms and tornados. As artists and photographers continue to notice, the land is often blessed with deep—blue cloudless skies whose majestic sunsets are characterized by brilliant reds, oranges, and yellows that reign unimpeded over a vast horizon. Many say those sunsets compensate for any and all of the more uncomfortable elements that nature asks West Texans to endure.

THE WIND GAUGE

Ask most any West Texan about the constancy of the wind, and he will probably tell you that most days it only blows about thirty or forty miles per hour, but sometimes it really picks up. The truth of such exaggeration is that to strangers trying to adapt, it seems just that harsh and unrelenting. And from the earliest days of settlement, the wind has been as perpetual a source of stories as it has been of sandstorms.

Take the one about the would-be speculator intent on buying up inexpensive land. He happened upon an isolated sod house way out on the prairie where he was invited to spend the night. Over supper with the homesteader and his family, the conversation turned to the weather and more particularly to the wind howling mournfully around the corner of the house. The stranger inquired how the family coped with the constant moaning. The homesteader explained that they had grown so used to it that they scarcely heard it anymore. "Of course," he cautioned, "only a fool would become too complacent." He himself had rigged a warning device for high winds. Would his guest like to see it? When the speculator nodded, the homesteader showed him a small hole in the wall near the front door. "Every morning," he explained, "I poke a crow bar through that hole. If it's bent when I pull it back in, we don't venture out that day."

SANDSTORM JOURNEY

As large a role as sandstorms continue to play on the plains of West Texas, they are subdued incarnations of their predecessors in the 1930s and 1950s. My folks tell me that they were so bad back in the '30s that chickens, thinking it was night, often went to roost at midday. I can't swear to the events of the '30s, but I was eyeball witness to the sandstorms of the '50s.

In 1954 I made a trip of some eighty-odd miles with my friend Billy Bob in a newly purchased Ford coupe that was his pride and joy. Our trip took us westerly from Odessa into the teeth of a raging sandstorm. The further we went, the worse it got. By the time we reached Carlsbad, our destination, the sand was so thick that we could barely see past the hood ornament. Next morning, after the wind had died down, we discovered that the blowing sand had scoured all the paint off the front of that new car, and the bumper was pitted beyond repair. Billy Bob was inconsolable. Almost.

The company of the young women we'd journeyed to visit did quite a bit for his spirits, and as it turned out the paintless front end of the car turned out to be a blessing in disguise. The girls were fascinated by the fury of the storm we'd braved, which became all the more dangerous in the telling. All in all, our ordeal made for a much more romantic interlude. In fact things were going so well that on the day of our return, we were delayed until well after dark. That proved to be our undoing.

We were sunk if we didn't make it back in time for the graveyard shift, so Billy Bob decided our only hope was to drive like a "bat out of Sunday school." Although barreling along a winding little two-lane in excess of ninety didn't do much to relieve my anxiety, there was absolutely no traffic, and I was beginning to think Billy Bob might be right. Then we met that oilfield-pipe truck.

The approaching headlights revealed what daylight hadn't, that the windshield was as pitted as the bumper. But even if I'd paid attention in physics, I wouldn't have predicted the effect of those high beams refracting on hundreds of tiny depressions in the glass.

What I recall is the windshield becoming a crystalline smear of blinding light that blanked out everything else in front of us, including the next curve in the road. I also remember us both going airborne, and the thud of landing, but after that it gets fairly hazy. While they were sewing me up in that little country hospital, the highway patrol told us that it was lucky we wound up in that cow lot. The manure absorbed most of the force of impact and probably saved our lives, although it didn't do much for our, uh, aura.

Our sandstorm experience may not have been too isolated in that era. Historians record that the 1950s were boom times for West Texas body shops and glass replacement businesses.

FREE ELECTRICITY

Even thornier than the breathing and visual problems associated with blowing sand is the phenomenon of static electricity. It seems all those tiny sand particles rubbing around on one another create a considerable electrical charge. I remember working on an oil-field tank one spring when a particularly bad sandstorm built up such a large static charge that streaks of electricity were leaping across the two-foot opening of the clean-out box. Every time we entered or left the vessel, our hair stood out in every direction and we received a small electrical shock accompanied by a loud pop. Nobody got electrocuted, but it sure made us all nervous.

Of course that was nothing compared to the experience of Walter, a lease pumper who lived out around Iraan back in the '30s. It seems this fellow had a natural mind for scientific inquiry and no qualms whatsoever about siphoning off something the company sure didn't need. After studying the problem a while, he figured out how to harness the electrical charges playing around some of the tank batteries, and darned if he didn't use it to electrify the little lease house where he lived with his family. Before long they were enjoying all the modern conveniences that electricity could afford. They even had a radio that could pick up the Grand Ole Opry all the way from Nashville. By the standards of that time and place, the little family was living in the lap of luxury. Then one day an unusually strong sandstorm blew up. It was one of those wall clouds that blackened the horizon and enveloped everything in its path. With it came an overabundance of static electricity probably enough to power a small village. Unfortunately old Walter's system had no provision for bleeding off the excess charge, and faster than you could hear a pop, the system overloaded. Before Walter could do anything, that jerry-rigged mass of wires, capacitors, and assorted other electrical devices shorted out, exploding a bank of twenty-four storage batteries and burning up 20,000 barrels of oil. The surge alone barbecued a side of beef right in Walter's fancy new deep freeze and singed all the hair off his wife's head. From that day forward, Walter and his family had no truck with rural electrification.

THE SAWMILL

Once I interviewed an old man out in Monahans who claimed to have arrived before the sawmills left. When I questioned how such a dry climate ever supported large stands of timber, he gave me one of those pitying looks with which senior citizens suffer the ignorance of youth. Then with a sigh he began to explain. It seems he was working at a sawmill back in East Texas when the boss approached him about the operations cranking up in that sandy country over in Winkler County, where there was suddenly a timber surplus. The prospects seemed too promising to ignore, so the millworker packed up and moved west.

The way he told it out around Wink and Kermit, the sand blew so constantly from the southwest that it drifted up over the telephone and utility poles. To stay ahead of that problem, linemen devised means of clamping new poles to the tops of nearly buried ones and raising the endangered lines out of harm's way. In some places those poles stood three or four deep.

Then, owing to some meteorological fluke that no one could explain, the winds in Winkler County reversed, slowly but surely uncovering the lower poles. Without tons of sand pressing against them, the exposed joints were dangerously unstable, and the county's liability became the lumberman's bonanza. The utility company moved swiftly to lower all the lines to their original height, so the now superfluous poles could be harvested for lumber before they toppled. Enterprising sawmillers rushed in to take advantage.

A spate of new mills ran day and night, producing who knows how many board feet of high-grade lumber. Then just as mysteriously as it had before, the winds shifted again. Dryland crops to the south and west failed—as they will in such country—and record highs, drought, and thermals conspired to carry half of New Mexico into Winkler County, burying the poles again, foot by foot. And that, the old man concluded, was the end of the West Texas timber rush.

ONE-UPSMANSHIP

Urban legends have nothing on the stories told in the cafés and gin offices of rural West Texas, especially when it comes to weather. Every community, no matter how small, has someplace where regulars gather to have their morning coffee and swap exaggerations. If you want to hear some first-rate storytelling, that is the place to find it.

Once when I was gathering oral histories from old oil-field hands over around Breckenridge, I stopped in a café where the conversation had turned to tornadoes. Everybody had his favorite story. One related his miraculous escape from a trailer house picked up and twisted in half by a funnel. Another related the old story of a straw being blown through a telephone pole just like a bullet, only the pole was on his uncle's place of course. Then someone told about the righteous tornado that spared a bootlegger's house but destroyed the homes of three Baptist deacons and the local preacher who lived on either side of the bootlegger. The yarn spinning went on until an old gentleman, tiring of the competition, soberly took the floor.

Tornadoes, he reminded them, were no joking matter. As a young man he was living just outside of Lueders when a tornado struck late one afternoon. It was a terrible disaster. The entire town was destroyed with the exception of, yes, a lone structure in the center of town, the Catholic Church. And yes, there were straws sticking out of telephone poles like quills on a porcupine. The important thing was that despite the devasta-

tion, they dug out hundreds of survivors from buried storm cellars. The next morning as he joined others surveying the damage, he heard a muffled rooster's crow. At first it seemed to be coming from a pile of rubble, but as he dug about in the debris, the origin of the sound seemed to shift. The storyteller spent the better part of the morning trying to find that rooster, but to no avail.

That night the mystery bothered him so that he could hardly sleep. In the morning he returned to the site, determined to comb it systematically. Although the rooster kept crowing, the man still couldn't pinpoint his location. Finally, in exasperation, he kicked a narrow-mouthed whiskey jug he'd just unearthed, hard enough to shatter it. Out popped the rooster, still crowing.

"Top that one if you can," said the old man as he exited without waiting for rebuttal.

HOTTER 'N PECOS

West Texas summers can get unmercifully hot. That was certainly the case the last one I worked in the oil patch. We spent most of that summer on a big job down on the Rocker B, a little north of Big Lake. The temperature hovered slightly over, under, and around the hundred-degree mark from June through August. I don't recall a single rain to cool things off. One day at noon I was griping about the heat when "Little Red" looked over, gave me one of his lopsided grins, and admitted that it was indeed hot. But he allowed that it was nowhere near as miserable as that sandy country down on the Pecos a little distance below Imperial.

"Now I'm here to tell you," he pronounced, "It gets hot down on the Pecos."

He recounted working down there back in the early '50s and how they'd go through a five-gallon water can per man every day just to keep heat strokes at bay. It was so hot the sweat ran down into their work boots, sloshed around, and squished out the tops, compelling them to change their socks three or four times a day. It eventually got so bad that they considered leaving the six-packs of beer out of the water cans, which would have been rank foolishness. Instead, they began leaving the house early enough each morning to start work at first light. That way they were able to lie up in the shade of the truck for a couple of hours during the hottest part of the day. It was during one of those respites that "Little Red" began to study the local wildlife.

The first thing that caught his attention was the unusual activity of the lizards. There was a bunch of them in that sandy ground along the river. Usually, when you spot a lizard, it is scurrying along in a big hurry. These were doing that all right, but they all had this strange gait and what looked to be unusually large mouth parts. Red finally figured out that what he was seeing was not their mouths at all but little sticks they were carrying as they ran like blazes across the hot sand. When they couldn't stand the heat any longer, they spit out those sticks and jumped up on them to cool their little tootsies.

When he finished the story, "Little Red" looked me right in the eye and with the straightest of faces exclaimed, "It don't get no hotter 'n Pecos!"

THE GOOFY ROOFERS

A Study in Free Enterprise

As best as I can remember it all started back in the spring of '64. I was working at one of those petrochemical plants on the south side of Odessa when a tremendous hail storm hit and ruined most of the roofs in town. Three of us hands from the plant pitched in and helped Gene repair his roof. It worked out so well that we decided we might as well get into the roofing business and make some of that sure money. So the Goofy Roofers, as we came to be known, came into existence.

In truth, the four of us—Frank, Don, Gene, and I—knew about as much about roofing as a pig does about flying. But we had observed some roofers in action, and to us geniuses the work seemed fairly simple minded—a descriptor that fitted us to a tee.

The prevalent roof style in our part of West Texas was a low-pitched affair in keeping with the ranch-style homes. We called them tar and gravel roofs because they were constructed by putting down a layer of tar paper on which a coating of tar was spread to accept a layer of gravel. The only trick was making sure that you spread the gravel quickly, before the tar hardened, so it would be sure to adhere. Laid properly, these roofs could last for years in that dry climate. Interested as we were in conservation (of our own labor and expense, that is), we were quick to discover that we could dispense with the tar-paper portion of the process by sweeping off as much of the remaining gravel as possible and washing the original tar paper clean, before applying a new coat of tar and gravel. It worked like a charm.

Within a couple of days of forming our little enterprise, Frank had sold a dozen or so roofing jobs. Our first order of business was the acquisition of equipment. Somehow, the two heavy-duty warehouse brooms and square-pointed shovels that we brought into the partnership didn't seem adequate capitalization for a business of that magnitude. Accordingly, we voted to put up $100 each and open a company bank account. Before long Don spotted an old abandoned tar pot in a vacant lot on the edge of town. We salvaged the thing and managed to get it operating. Next, Gene bought a steel horse trailer with the top cut off. It looked for all the world like one of those Roman chariots you see in the movies, but it could haul a couple of tons of gravel if you aired up the tires really well. At that point we were good to go.

We all worked the same rotating shifts at the plant: seven daylights, two days off; seven evenings, two days off; seven graveyards, three days off. We could complete a roof a day while working evenings and graveyards and at least two roofs per day on our days off. On one memorable occasion we even finished four roofs in one day. When working daylights we didn't do any roofing, but we did manage to sell a bunch of jobs during those shifts. Boy, how the money rolled in!

I'll never forget our first dividend distribution. It happened on one of our days off. We set the tar pot to heating in an alley early that morning and while it was getting up to temperature, we all piled into a car and went down to the bank. We drew out $8,000 in $100 bills and stopped for coffee at a café where we divided the money. There we sat in one of those Naugahyde booths, in our tar-stained jeans, while Frank counted out the money like he was dealing a hand of poker. The waitress stood

there watching us with eyes as big as saucers, and when we finished we paid for our coffee and left a three-cent tip. That was all the extra cash the four of us had on us, and we sure weren't going to leave one of the hundreds.

By the time we got back within a mile of the roofing job that morning, we could see a plume of black smoke rising into the sky. The fire truck turned into the alley just ahead of us. They managed to quench the flames engulfing our primary capital asset in jig time. It was a sorry sight. Tar was dripping off the pot in streams, and one tire had burned off causing the machine to list sharply to starboard. Things looked pretty grim, but on the bright side, we hadn't burned down any fences or houses; the exterior of the pot was as clean as a whistle now that the excess tar had burned off, and the tar in the pot was piping hot. We decided to go ahead and roof the house before the tar cooled. Considering what might have happened, things worked out just fine.

We put a used tire on the pot, made a few other minor repairs, and were back in apple-pie order. We were ready for another capital investment—a ten-year-old half-ton International pickup. It wasn't much to look at and was geared down so low that it never managed to exceed fifty miles per hour, but it would haul as much gravel as you could stack on it. (Word of warning to those in the market for one of those vehicles: the left-side lug bolts on an International are threaded to the left and the right-side bolts are threaded to the right. We could have used that bit of information, although the little bitty L on the end of the left side bolts should have tipped us off. Did you know that a man can twist off one of those bolts while changing a tire if he gets on it hard enough?)

Our little enterprise grew phenomenally that spring and summer. We replaced the original tar pot with a much larger two-burner machine that greatly enhanced our productivity. The operational learning curve was a little steeper on that two-burner than on its predecessor, singeing off my eyebrows and lashes and searing my face into a red balloon. But by the time the swelling went down and the hair grew back, I had that pesky blow-back problem solved, and work proceeded on schedule.

Nonetheless, you can ride a weather phenomenon like that hail storm only so far. By the onset of cold weather, the boom had pretty well subsided. By spring we were seriously considering liquidating all our capital assets when lo and behold there came another massive hail storm. This time it hit Midland, only twenty miles away. We rushed to the scene of the crime and began to ply our roofing trade at another venue. This time, however, Don opted out of the scheme, leaving only three of us to carry on the tradition of the Goofy Roofers.

In Midland we discovered one of those little cul-de-sac streets that contained about forty residences. I don't recollect its name, but we dubbed it Money Street because we sold every house a roof job. By the time we finished that area we had branched out into doing churches and a variety of other types of large structures. Business could not have been better.

At that point fate intervened in the form of medical disability. I developed a severe allergy to the fumes of melting tar. That was not a good thing in our line of work. It culminated one hot July morning, causing me to broach the subject of selling my part of the business to Gene and Frank. At the time we were about half finished with roofing a small home on the west side of Midland. Over lunch we negotiated a deal for one-third of the value of all the capital assets plus one-third of all outstanding invoices. They hauled out the company checkbook from under the seat of that old International pickup and wrote me a check for the agreed upon price right then and there.

Afterward, Gene allowed that we might as well get back to work and finish the job we'd started that morning. I declined, reminding them, "I don't work for this chicken outfit anymore." I lay in the shade of a tree for most of the afternoon while they finished the roof but relented enough to help load the tools after the work was all done.

Although the Goofy Roofers lasted through that summer, owing to a lack of weather disasters it was never revived as a viable entity. Gene and Frank might say that it was just as well.

FROM WHENCE THEY CAME

This is supposed to be a small bibliographic essay of sorts, but the truth is that most of these stories came right out of my head.

The oil patch stories come from a variety of sources. I chose them because they relate much about the character of the oil-field hands I knew over the years. The "Tank Setter," "Tailing Rods," and "So You Want to Build a Museum Exhibit" yarns are purely from my personal experiences. Jimmy "Ziglo" Zeigler, whom I built tanks with for years, was a master storyteller, and among his many yarns is the basis for "The Roughneck's Tale" and a variety of others scattered throughout the book, including "Hotter 'n Pecos." I probably owe Ziglo as much credit as any other source for much of what appears in this book. "The Boll Weevil" is strung together from bits and pieces of stories that have been around forever about the hazing of new hands in the patch. I knew "Old Whitey" well in his later years, and his yarns and those others told on him are legion. Bill Bishop related to me his "Graduation Night," which I think points out the need many younger folk have for leaving the patch. "The Driller and the Monkey," "The Promoter," and "The Toughest Man in Oil Town" are stories that have made the rounds in the oil patch for generations in one form or another and have many variations. The "Nitro" story comes from several sources including one from John J. McLaurin's 1896 book entitled *Sketches in Crude Oil,* several interviews concerning "Tex" Thornton in my personal collection, and a yarn told to me by an old "shooter" from Wichita Falls whose name I cannot remember because we were consulting over a fifth of Wild Turkey at the time. "What's In a Name" is a little different. Over the years it has occurred to me that oil patch hands tend toward nicknames more than most, a perception borne out by numerous references to the practice in the oral histories of the Pioneers of Texas Oil Collection at the Center for American History at the University of Texas. So I began to jot those names down as I came across them and over time that has developed into a considerable list. I thought it might be fun to do something with them.

The ranching stories also come from a variety of sources. "Firewood" and "The Wash Pan" are both yarns I heard J. Evetts Haley relate at various times over a period of years. Byron Price shared the story of "The Gate," which he said was also one of Mr. Haley's favorite stories. To the best of my knowledge none of those tales from the mouth of one of Texas's most knowledgeable historians on Texas ranching have ever appeared in print. My daddy told me the story of "Soap and Water," and my brother and his friends lived the "Legend of Black Question" experience back in their high school days. I knew Rex McQueen ("The Wolf Hunter") well and personally observed Old Gabe and Walker at their work on Old Man Sid Kyle's place out in Loving County. "The Bullfighter" is another incident that has its origin in truth, and if everything chronicled in the story didn't happen exactly that way, it should have.

The farming yarns that appear I heard from several people. I met "The Crop Duster" and heard his stories exactly as portrayed the first year I was at Texas Tech as an undergraduate. At the time we were taking botany but spent most of our time over at the Student Union Building, which ultimately caused him to have to repeat the course. There is a germ of truth in "The Cotton Patch" because my Uncle "Preach" did farm up on the Prairie Dog Town Fork of the Red River during the '50s and '60s. He eventually made three good crops in a row, sold out, and moved back to Central Texas. My brother Curt who tried pig farming right out of high school was pretty much the inspiration for "Hauling Hogs."

There are literally thousands of weather stories relating to West Texas. The only one in this collection that I did not personally collect is "One-Upsmanship" which is based on an interview with H.P. Nichols in the "Pioneers of Texas Oil Collection" at the Center for American History at the University of Texas. "The Wind Gauge" I heard in one form or another from a variety of sources over the years. "The Sandstorm Journey," "Free Electricity," and "The Sawmill" all come from a kernel of truth combined with Ziglo's help and my imagination.

"The Goofy Roofers" is, once again, autobiographical in nature. Gene Woodard, Frank Bush, Don Eubanks, and I did go into the roofing business and all the events related and a lot more actually happened. The name of the business was foisted off on us by the fellow workers on our regular job. All these things happened pretty much as I related in the stories. If you don't believe me I can point you to some guys who will verify them and a lot more if you have the time to listen.

Well, that pretty much sums up "From Whence They Came." The truth is they came from me and all those other West Texans that I met or heard about over the years. I think their yarns provide a pretty fair likeness of those who live out west of the hundredth.

976.49 W363   HPARW
Weaver, Bobby D.
Hotter 'n pecos and other west Texas
lies /
PARK PLACE
10/10